Buddy the Bass and the Gooey Green Slime
Copyright ©2022 Edwin Mark Brooks, Beaver Creek Lake Series.

ISBN Hardcover: 979-8-218-05096-2
ISBN Paperback: 979-8-218-05104-4
ISBN E-book: 979-8-218-05097-9

Magicmarkbrooks.com

BUDDY THE BASS

AND THE

GOOEY GREEN SLIME

WRITTEN BY **EDWIN MARK BROOKS**

ILLUSTRATED BY **EMILY DROUIN**

It was a sunny spring day in Beaver Creek Lake. Otis and Bethany Beaver tended to the dam while watching over their three kits playing with a twig near the den.

Otis is the mayor of the lake. He wins every election because well, he built the lake.

Bethany sang while patching a hole that just started leaking. "I can build a dam. I can chop a tree. I can slap my tail and scare my enemies!"

And with that, she slapped the water so hard the birds that were resting nearby suddenly flew away. She giggled.

SLAP!

Cuppy the Crawfish was building
the biggest mound he'd ever made.
He wanted to build a tower so big he could view all
of Beaver Creek Lake from the top. The problem was,
every time it rained his towers fell down
and he had to start all over again.

Cuppy sang while he worked,
"Mud...oh the mud. It's the muddiest mud I know!
When the rain comes down, well I don't frown
'cause I get to build again tomorrow!"

The entire lake was abuzz with the joy of
spring and duties of survival.

Most of the fish build nests in the shallows to lay eggs.
Not Buddy though, he hatched last year and all he wanted to do is play...and eat!

"Splash! Chomp! Splash!" Buddy lunged out of the water and nabbed
an unsuspecting grasshopper. "Yummy!" Buddy yelled. "I'm a predator
and predators hunt and eat and eat and hunt...and play."

Just then Cranky the Catfish slowly swam over to Buddy.
"What's all the racket? Can't an old catfish get some
shut-eye around here?" he said sternly.

Buddy didn't mind, he sassed, "I'm a predator and predators
hunt and eat and eat and hunt...and play!" Buddy flipped
his tail and disappeared from Cranky's sight.

"Well, that little fishtail!" Cranky grumbled.

At night the lake is so quiet. Unless you're listening to the million crickets chirping, bullfrogs croaking, coyotes barking, tree frogs chattering, the "Hoot!" of an owl or the "lap lap lap" of the water as the warm wind nudges it onto the bank of the lake. It's just beautiful. It's the best ecosystem ever!

What is an "eco-sys-tem", you ask? Why that is a big question!

You see, everything in Beaver Creek Lake depends on everything in Beaver Creek Lake to survive. The ecosystem includes every fish, bug, frog, crawfish, raccoon, bird, you, me...you name it. Even mud, water, and air are a part of it.

Everything around you whether it's alive or not is part of your ecosystem, even in your home. Oh...but if the ecosystem at Beaver Creek Lake is disturbed, if even one part of it is lost or sickened, all the creatures who live in Beaver Creek Lake could be no more. What would we do then?

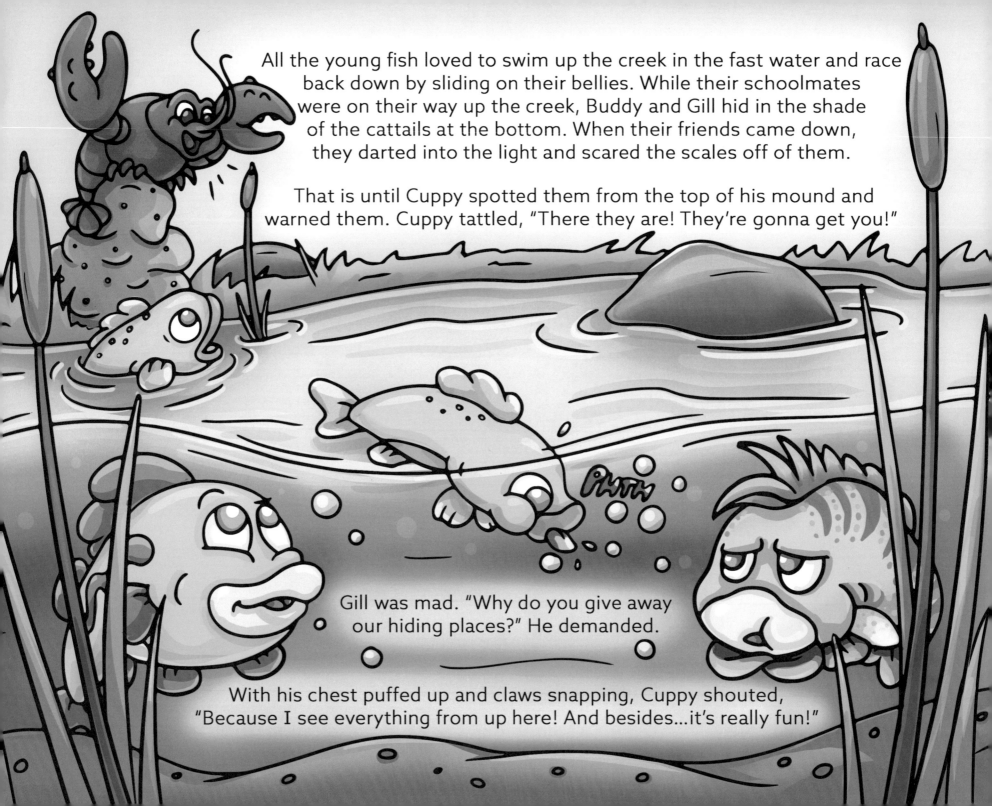

All the young fish loved to swim up the creek in the fast water and race back down by sliding on their bellies. While their schoolmates were on their way up the creek, Buddy and Gill hid in the shade of the cattails at the bottom. When their friends came down, they darted into the light and scared the scales off of them.

That is until Cuppy spotted them from the top of his mound and warned them. Cuppy tattled, "There they are! They're gonna get you!"

Gill was mad. "Why do you give away our hiding places?" He demanded.

With his chest puffed up and claws snapping, Cuppy shouted, "Because I see everything from up here! And besides...it's really fun!"

Later that day Cuppy wasn't feeling so good. He told Doctor Molly the Mockingbird, or Doc Mock as they called her, that he was building a new tower in Beaver Creek and it felt like something bit his tail.

"Does this hurt, Cuppy?" Doc Mock asked.
"Yes it does!" Cuppy shouted in pain.
"Well, it's a big green sore. We'll have to find out what caused this." She explained.

Doc Mock bandaged Cuppy's tail and immediately reported the news to Mayor Otis. He was eager to solve the mystery.

"If all of the diggers get sick it could spell disaster!" He said.
He called an emergency town meeting.

Mayor Otis told everyone about Cuppy's big green sore and what it could mean for their lake. "We need some brave fish to go up the creek and find out what's causing this sickness. Are there any volunteers?" Mayor Otis asked.

Buddy immediately volunteered, "I'm one of the best swimmers in the lake! I'll go up!" He said proudly.

Being cautious and concerned, Mayor Otis explained, "There is a fork in the creek. It'll take more than one brave fish to do this investigation. Who is brave enough to go with Buddy?" He asked.

"I'll go!" Gill touted. He'd never leave Buddy's side when there was a possibility of danger or adventure.

"We'll start bright and early in the morning then! I'll see you two at the base of the creek at first light." Mayor Otis told the boys.

The next morning many of the crawfish on the Northside were sick and very afraid. Their tails had bright green sores on them and they hurt badly. Whatever this was, it was extremely dangerous!

Mayor Otis was worried about Buddy and Gill, but there had to be answers.

. "It's okay, Mayor Otis", Buddy said, "We'll be safe and look for anything unusual and report back."

"Yeah." Gill snorted, "Anything unusual!"

Mayor Otis shouted, "Whatever you find up there, don't touch it!" Buddy and Gill headed up the creek.

Buddy swam like a champ when suddenly, "Ouch!" something bit his fin! It really hurt but Buddy stopped right there and held his position in the fast-moving water. He saw something bright green that was dripping into the creek.

"That's got to be it!" He said to himself.

He swam further upstream to get a better look. There was a pipe and it was dripping something really gooey, bright green, and extremely slimy! He looked at his hurt fin, "Yip, bright green and really sore!"

Buddy belly slid back down to the fork as fast as he could.

"Hey! Wait!" Buddy heard. He turned around and there was Gill. "I'm really sick. Can you help me back down?" Gill pleaded.

"Yes, I've got you, Gill. We're gonna get through this!" Buddy said. The two made their way back down as best they could.

"They've made it back!" Mayor Otis shouted to everyone.
Doc Mock immediately began tending to Gill who was really sick.

Buddy was out of breath but explained, "There was a pipe... there was gooey
green slime coming out of it. That's got to be what's causing the sickness!"

"I'll look at your fin next, Buddy." Dock Mock said as she tended to Gill.

She continued, "We need an aerial view to see where that pipe goes.
Let's get everyone who feels sick to the Southside of the lake in the calm water
and I'll fly over and find that pipe. I'll come right back with the info
and we can try to figure out what to do next."

Everyone did as she'd instructed. She headed upstream and flew as fast as her wings could carry her. Sure enough, there was the pipe. There was a sign on a building that read, "Monetary Chemical Company". Then she saw another pipe that went all the way over to the stream Gill had been in and it was dripping gooey green slime, too! She brought the news back to the lake.

It seemed safe on the Southside of the lake at least for now, but no one was sure what to do. Buddy, Gill, and the crawfish were beginning to feel better but were extremely worried. There was nowhere else they could live. What were they to do?

MCC MONETARY CHEMICAL COMPANY

"Are we all doomed?" Cuppy asked.

They knew that sooner or later the whole lake would be infected with the gooey green slime and that they could all die. They needed a miracle and fast.

A few days later, Buddy was resting near the edge of the water. He was feeling better but was worried about what the future held.

"Fetch, Zep!" a man wearing a big floppy tan hat yelled after throwing an orange float out in the lake.

KERSPLUNK!

Just inches away from Buddy, Zep, a big beautiful dog, hurled into the lake and made a huge splash. Buddy hid and watched what was going on. Zep swam out, nabbed the orange float, and brought it back to the floppy-hatted man. They kept doing this over and over and Buddy began to get an idea.

He swam over to the nearest school of fish and said, "I've got an idea! Go tell Mayor Otis everything will be okay!"

Buddy hid near the floppy-hatted man and waited.
"Kersplunk!" the orange float hit the water.
"Splash!" and Zep was on his way.

Buddy raced Zep to the float and grabbed its rope in his mouth. He headed straight for Beaver Creek and the gooey green slime! Zep followed hot on his trail! Buddy pulled and tugged and tugged and pulled. Zep was getting close but Buddy kept swimming!

Buddy thought to himself, "I've got to show him the gooey green slime!"

Soon they were near the pipe of death and Zep made a dash for his float. He nabbed it! Buddy held on but was dragged right under the pipe in the fight!

"Ieep! Ieep! Ieep!" Zep cried loudly.

The gooey green slime had dripped right on Zep's head! He lunged out of the water and ran straight to the floppy-hatted man. He took Zep to the veterinarian as fast as he could. That's where humans take their dogs when they're sick.

The gooey green slime had dripped on Buddy, too! Between the race to the top and the pain of the gooey green slime, he passed out and slowly drifted back down to the lake. He was barely alive when Gill found him.

"Hurry! Buddy needs Doc Mock!" Gill screamed.

Gill and some friends took him to the Southside of the lake and got Doc Mock. Buddy was in bad shape.

A few days later there was a commotion on the lake. There were people wearing shiny-looking suits walking around everywhere. They had machines and tools, and they were putting water into small tubes. Some of them were in scuba gear and swam to the bottom of the lake. They dug deep into the soil and put it in buckets. They marched up the creek and found the pipes and the gooey green slime!

Bethany Beaver was hiding nearby and heard one of the workers say, "If it hadn't been for that dog finding those pipes, this lake and all the wildlife here would have been lost."

No more gooey green slime came out of the pipes after that day and chains were placed on the doors of the building. The words, "Permanently Closed" had been painted over the Monetary Chemical Company sign. A note was left on the door that said, "Building is scheduled for destruction and clean up."

Soon the entire Beaver Creek Lake area would be safe for all the wildlife again.

A few weeks later, Buddy, his friends, and the entire lake were back to normal.
Cuppy shouted from the top of his biggest tower yet,
"They're hatching! All of them! Baby fish everywhere!
Just look!"

Beaver Creek Lake rejoiced. It was the happiest of days!

Just then, Cuppy saw Buddy hiding in the shade of the tall cattails.
"There he is!" He yelled, "Hiding in the shade! The one Mayor Otis
proclaimed Guardian of Beaver Creek Lake...Buddy the Bass!"

Buddy didn't move, he waited...until the perfect moment
as old Cranky slowly swam by and then..."Boo!"

"Why I oughta!" Cranky complained, "You little fishtail!"
All of the residents of Beaver Creek Lake laughed...
oh...except Cranky of course.

The townspeople made all of Beaver Creek and Beaver Creek Lake a protected wildlife area and park, making sure future generations could enjoy the fresh air, clean water, and natural wildlife.

They even erected a sign where the evil company's pipes had polluted the creek with the gooey green slime. It's a picture of Zep with the float in his mouth and a bandage on his head. It reads, "This is Zep, Hero of Beaver Creek Town. He saved Beaver Creek and its Lake by leading us to the evil polluters – Monetary Chemical Company."

BEAVER CREEK WILDLIFE PRESERVE & PARK

THIS IS ZEP, HERO OF BEAVER CREEK TOWN. HE SAVED BEAVER CREEK AND ITS LAKE BY LEADING US TO THE EVIL POLLUTERS - MONETARY CHEMICAL COMPANY.

All of the lake dwellers knew whose picture should have really been on that sign, but they were glad Zep was okay. Without him, they may have all died.

BUDDY THE BASS

AND THE

GOOEY GREEN SLIME

WRITTEN BY **EDWIN MARK BROOKS**

ILLUSTRATED BY **EMILY DROUIN**

BUDDY'S

Hannah Bagwell

Liana Baskett

Victor Baskett

Sophie Breitrick

Eli Brooks

Tanner Brooks

Novalee Jewell

Arya Jewell

August Jewell

Olivia Kirkwood

Karsyn Losser

Bobbi Jo Marx

Cynthia Thomas

Kaitlyn Thurby

Caleb Waterstram

Jacob Waterstram

Stephen Westby

BUDDIES

Liliana Butcher

Lola Campbell

Natalie Cusato

Jaiden Davis

Arrington Gogel

Maxwell Mazza

Rowan Mazza

Talon Norvel

Grayson Orourke

Brandon Owens

Lindsey James Williams

Tessa C. Williams

...and you! _ _ _ _ _ _ _ _

(your name)

Lightning Source UK Ltd.
Milton Keynes UK
UKRC031042131022
410418UK00001B/2